The case of the

Dumb
Bells

The case of the

Dumb Bells

An I Can Read Book®

HarperTrophy®
A Division of HarperCollins Publishers

by Crosby Bonsall

Library of Congress Catalog Card Number: 66-8267
ISBN 0-06-444030-3 (pbk.)
First Harper Trophy edition, 1982.

for Dinah

Skinny got a telephone set
at the junk store.

Wizard and his brother Snitch
didn't get a tclephone set.

Tubby didn't get a telephone set.

7

And they were friends.

They were pals.

They stuck together

through thick and thin.

But Skinny had a telephone set

and they didn't.

8

Skinny said,

"We can hook it up

to our clubhouse.

We are private eyes,

and we need a telephone."

They were friends, all right.

They were pals.

They stuck together

through thick and thin.

All the way home

Skinny told them

how he could hook up

the wires in his cellar.

He would

bring the wires across the lot

to the clubhouse

in Wizard and Snitch's yard.

It would be easy as pie.

Tubby had a big, long face.

"Skinny has a phone," he said.

"Wizard and Snitch

will have a phone.

What about me?

I'm a private eye too!"

"There's another phone
in the junk store," Skinny said.
"But nobody has any money,"
said Wizard.
"Maybe we could earn the money,"
Skinny said.

13

Wizard minded the kids across the street.

Tubby ran errands for the baker.

Skinny walked four dogs and a cat.

And Snitch sold lemonade.

When they had enough money,

they went to the junk store.

"Know how to hook up these sets?"

the man asked.

"Oh, sure," Skinny said.

"It's easy. Easy as pie."

18

Skinny worked out a plan.

He put name tapes on one phone.

SKINNY on one button,

TUBBY on the other button.

That was the clubhouse phone.

Tubby and Skinny could only call

the clubhouse on their telephones.

19

Skinny hooked up wires

in his cellar.

He hooked up wires

in Tubby's cellar.

He carried the wires

across the yard to the clubhouse.

"Will it work?" Snitch asked.

"Oh, sure," Skinny said.

"It was easy as pie.

Now, if you want to call Tubby,

push the TUBBY button.

If you want to call me,

push the SKINNY button."

Skinny went home to test the phone.

Buzz. Wizard answered.

"Testing," he said.

"I said it was easy as pie,"

cried Skinny

on the other end of the line.

The phone worked!

Tubby ran home to try his phone.

Buzz. Snitch said, "Testing."

"Boy, that Skinny is great,"

cried Tubby

on the other end of the line.

23

Next morning Snitch called Tubby.

He pushed the TUBBY button.

Tubby did not answer.

He pushed the SKINNY button.

Skinny did not answer.

He tried again. Nobody answered.

Just then Tubby came over.

"Listen," he said.

"Something funny

is going on around here!

Our doorbell has been ringing."

"Big deal," Wizard said.

25

"But nobody is at the door!"

Tubby cried.

Wizard said, "It's some kid
playing tricks. Call Skinny.
Maybe he's the one."

Skinny didn't answer.

"Nobody *ever* answers," said Snitch.

Just then Skinny ran across the yard.

"Listen," he cried.

"Something funny

is going on around here!"

"We know. We know," Wizard said.

"Your doorbell has been ringing,

but nobody is there."

"How do you know?" Skinny asked.

"*Our* doorbell has been ringing,"

Tubby told him.

"It's some kid playing tricks,"

Wizard said.

The telephone buzzed.

"Wizard, private eye," Wizard said.

"Yes, Mom. You're at Skinny's house?

Yes, Mom. Okay, Mom.

'Bye, Mom."

Wizard hung up.

"Mom wants me,"

he told the kids.

When Wizard came back, he said,

"Listen, men,

we have to find out

who's ringing those doorbells.

We have to find out *right now!*

We're private eyes.

And private eyes find people—

people who ring doorbells!"

"You said it was some kid,"

Skinny said.

"Why don't you think so now?"

Tubby asked.

"Mom thinks it was us,"

Wizard said.

"I told her

we wouldn't do a thing like that!

But she's pretty mad."

The telephone buzzed.

"Wizard, private eye," Wizard said.

"Just a minute, please. For you, Tub."

Tubby said, "Hello?

Yes, Mom. No, Mom.

No, honest, Mom. Yes, Mom."

Tubby hung up.

"Boy, is Mom mad!" Tubby said.

"The doorbell rang

two more times.

Her cake is all burned,

and she thinks it's us."

"Dumb old bells," Snitch said.

The telephone buzzed.

Skinny picked it up.

"Skinny, private eye," he said.

"Hello, Pop. Yes, Pop.

No, we didn't, Pop. Yes, we will, Pop.

Sorry, Pop." And he hung up.

"Boy, is Pop mad!" Skinny said.

"He's taking a bath,

the doorbell keeps ringing,

and my mother is over at

Tubby's house."

"I don't like baths," Snitch said.

"Yes, but Pop does," Skinny said.

"And he's dripped downstairs
four times this morning.

He thinks it's us!"

"Those dumb old bells," Snitch said.

"Well, let's look around, men,"
Wizard said.

"Snitch, you stay by the phone.

But don't use it.

We may have to call you."

Tubby followed

a tall, thin man

who might ring doorbells.

But he didn't.

Skinny followed

a short, fat man

who might ring doorbells.

But he didn't.

Wizard followed a man with a bag

who might ring doorbells.

The man with a bag

rang doorbells.

But he waited until the lady came.

The kids met again

at the clubhouse.

The telephone buzzed.

It was for Tubby.

"Yes, Mom? *Seventeen times!*

Wow! Yes, Mom." He hung up.

"Boy, are we in trouble!"

Tubby cried.

"The doorbell rang

seventeen times,

there's no cake for supper,

and the meat burned!"

The telephone buzzed again.

It was for Skinny.

"Yes, Pop. No kidding!

I mean, gee, Pop.

Seventeen times, Pop?

Boy! Yes, Pop. Yes, Pop."

He hung up.

"There's no hot water left,"
Skinny said.

"And there's a leak in the floor
of the bathroom,
and the water dripped through
on Mom's best rug.
We are in TROUBLE!"

Wizard had been thinking.

"We're doing it wrong," he said.

"We should be watching

your houses.

That's where the trouble is."

46

Tubby and Snitch

watched Skinny's front door.

There was a dog on the steps.

But he didn't ring the bell.

"Dumb old bells," said Snitch.

Skinny and Wizard

watched Tubby's front door.

There was a newspaper on the mat.

But the newspaper

didn't ring the bell.

On their way back

to the clubhouse

they heard the buzz

of the telephone

clear across the yard.

It buzzed and buzzed and buzzed.

Wizard and Snitch

ran like anything.

Tubby and Skinny

walked slowly.

"It's *my* pop," Skinny told Tubby,

"or *your* mom."

It was Skinny's pop.

"You were in the cellar, Pop?

Just a minute, please, Pop."

Skinny turned to the kids.

"This is a private call," he said.

The kids could still hear Skinny.

"Sure, Pop, I know

a doorbell wire

when I see one. Sure I do!

I don't?

But Pop . . . but Pop . . . but Pop."

"Gee, Pop. I'm sorry, Pop.

Yes, I hear you, Pop.

Pop?

Pop?

Pop?"

Skinny hung up.

Wizard was mad at Snitch.

"I told you to stay off that phone
this morning," Wizard said.

"You must have been
sitting on those buttons!"

54

The case was solved.

Now they all knew.

"Easy as pie, huh?"

Wizard said.

"I thought we were friends,"

said Skinny.

"No cake for supper," Tubby said.

"I thought we were pals,"
said Skinny.

"Dumb old bells," Snitch said.

"I thought we stuck together
through thick and thin," said Skinny.

Now Skinny was mad.
"A fine bunch of pals
you turned out to be!
Next time you can hook up
your old phones yourselves!"

Wizard felt like a rat.

Tubby felt like a rat.

Snitch felt like a rat.

"I'm a dumb old rat," Snitch said.

60

"Anybody can make a mistake,"

Wizard said.

"It's easy to make a mistake."

"That's right," said Snitch.

"It's easy as pie."

"Gee whiz," Tubby said,

"I wasn't hungry anyway.

Besides, I have a candy bar.

Want some?"

"That's okay," Skinny said.

They were friends.

They were pals.

They stuck together

through thick and thin.

Most of the time.